Thomas

KIDS CAN'T STOP READING
THE CHOOSE YOUR
OWN ADVENTURE® STORIES!

"Choose Your Own Adventure is the best thing that has come along since books themselves."
—Alysha Beyer, age 11

"I didn't read much before, but now I read my Choose Your Own Adventure books almost every night."
—Chris Brogan, age 13

"I love the control I have over what happens next."
—Kosta Efstathiou, age 17

"Choose Your Own Adventure books are so much fun to read and collect—I want them all!"
—Brendan Davin, age 11

And teachers like this series, too:

"We have read and reread, worn thin, loved, loaned, bought for others, and donated to school libraries our Choose Your Own Adventure books."

CHOOSE YOUR OWN ADVENTURE®—
AND MAKE READING MORE FUN!

Bantam Books in the Choose Your Own Adventure® Series
Ask your bookseller for the books you have missed

RETURN TO ATLANTIS

BY R.A. MONTGOMERY

ILLUSTRATED BY GEORGE TSUI

BANTAM BOOKS
TORONTO • NEW YORK • LONDON • SYDNEY • AUCKLAND

RL 4, IL age 10 and up

RETURN TO ATLANTIS
A Bantam Book / April 1988

CHOOSE YOUR OWN ADVENTURE® *is a registered trademark of
Bantam Books. Registered in U.S. Patent and Trademark
Office and elsewhere.*

Original conception of Edward Packard
Interior illustrations by George Tsui
Cover art by Catherine Huerta

ISBN 0-553-27123-7

Published simultaneously in the United States and Canada

*Bantam Books are published by Bantam Books, a division of Bantam
Doubleday Dell Publishing Group, Inc. Its trademark, consisting of the
words "Bantam Books" and the portrayal of a rooster, is Registered in U.S.
Patent and Trademark Office and in other countries. Marca Registrada.
Bantam Books, 666 Fifth Avenue, New York, New York 10103.*

PRINTED IN THE UNITED STATES OF AMERICA

O   0 9 8 7 6 5 4 3 2

RETURN TO ATLANTIS

WARNING!!!

Do not read this book straight through from beginning to end. These pages contain many different adventures you can have as you journey under the sea. From time to time as you read along, you will be asked to make a choice. Your choice may lead to success or disaster!

The adventures you take are a result of your choice. You are responsible because you choose! After you make your choice follow the instructions to see what happens to you next.

Be careful! Though three years have passed since your last visit to the Lost City of Atlantis, your journey under the sea will still be very dangerous.

Good luck!

"I want to go back. I really want to go back," you say out loud, thinking that you're alone in your office at the National Undersea Lab.

"Go back where?" asks a voice.

You spin around in your chair and see your research partner and closest friend standing in the doorway smiling at you.

"You know where. Back to Atlantis, where else?" you reply. "Come on in."

Horton James III enters the office, which is jammed with books, equipment, sharks' jaws, bottled squid, sea snakes, pieces of coral, and a large, rusted anchor. Horton removes a pile of magazines from a chair and sits down.

"So, the lure of the undersea world of Atlantis has got you again, has it? Once is not enough for our young hero? You *do* know that everyone thought you were suffering from hallucinations caused by being underwater too long when you were on that African excursion three years ago. Don't you?"

Turn to page 2.

2

You start to protest, then shrug your shoulders. No one has ever believed that you were really in the Lost City of Atlantis three years ago. After all, when you finally came back to the surface after being gone for several days, you carried no solid piece of evidence that you had found Atlantis and lived with the Atlanteans. People said you'd probably lain around in your undersea research craft, the *Seeker*, for those three days, delirious or hallucinating. Even the television reporters who interviewed you had winked at one another and listened to your story with barely concealed smiles.

Turn to page 8.

Three weeks later you and Horton are aboard the *Maray* in the middle of the ocean. You order the crew to bring the ship to a halt and to drop a sea anchor. The sea is an oily green, with just the hint of a swell, which rocks the ship gently. The *Seeker II*, painted a bright yellow, sits on its wooden crib. There's room enough inside the submarine for you and Horton plus gear for exploration outside the *Seeker II*.

"Here we go," you say, climbing into the *Seeker II*. Horton joins you, and you lock the hatch. Faintly you hear the whine of the winches lifting the *Seeker II* from its crib, and then you feel the submarine plunge into the sea. There's no cable attaching the submersible to the *Maray*. You and Horton are on your own.

The *Seeker II* glides down into an increasingly dark yet luminous world. It reminds you of dreams, some of them happy, some of them like nightmares.

"Lights on," you say in a light tone as you hit the search and probe buttons. The searchlights pick out fish, many of which dart away, startled by the light. You're looking at a world of gracefulness and beauty that hypnotizes and enchants you.

Turn to page 7.

4

"Horton," you shout, "we're going to dive!"

Horton comes out of his trance. "No! Don't dive! Don't dive!" he pleads. "I want to see what this thing is. It's beautiful—the sound and the music are beautiful."

"You're crazy. We can't waste any time."

With a sudden movement, you hit the red knob on the ceiling of the *Seeker II*. It's the emergency-dive control. You hear a loud hiss as compressed air rushes out of the fore and aft dive tanks. Aided by two booster jets, the *Seeker II* begins a rapid drop. Despite the intense pressure at 2,000 feet, the *Seeker II* accelerates, reaching 2,500 feet, then 2,700 feet, then 3,000 feet.

"Watch it!" Horton screams, pointing to a jagged column of rock in your path.

"I can't do anything! The descent is too rapid. We're going to crash."

"Try something!" Horton shouts. The jagged rocks are less than one hundred yards below you.

"Okay," you gasp, pushing the port-side booster jet to full force and tilting the diving planes to maximum side-slip angle.

The *Seeker II* shudders with the rapid moves. There's a grating, grinding noise as it glances off the side of the rock and slips along the edge of the mass.

Turn to page 15.

"Permission granted. You may come aboard. Please identify yourself and state how you propose to enter the *Seeker II,*" you say in a voice rising with excitement.

"We have technology capable of allowing us to transmit our energy and tranform shape and space. You will not be disturbed in the slightest."

You look at Horton, who seems to be completely wrapped up in recording and analyzing the music. A computer displays the sound waves, and Horton is comparing them to sound-wave patterns of whales and dolphins.

"Amazing, simply amazing," he says, carefully matching sets of patterns with the incoming musical sound waves.

"What's amazing?" you ask.

"The waves match! Whatever is out there is sending us whale music."

At that very instant, there's a change in the level and configuration of the incoming music.

Turn to page 24.

The *Seeker II* continues its descent. Then, suddenly, about a hundred yards in front of the submarine, you see an object so large it fills your entire range of vision. And it's breathing! At least it pulses in a way that indicates respiration.

"Yikes! What's that?" you whisper, afraid that if you speak too loudly, the thing will swallow the *Seeker II* in one massive gulp.

Attached to the side of the creature is a small silver capsule. It radiates a yellowish glow which seems to be blinking a signal to you. Below and to the starboard side of the *Seeker II* is a jumble of undersea rocks, and some small hills. This looks like the terrain where you found the entrance to Atlantis three years before.

Horton grabs your arm. "It's moving. Let's follow it," he says. "This could be the biggest fish story of all time."

You know that Horton's dying to investigate the beast, and it's *his* grant money that has made your trip possible. But something about this creature makes you wary—you have a feeling you'd better proceed with caution or avoid it altogether.

If you decide to track the beast, turn to page 20.

If you want to avoid the creature and descend into the territory where you believe the entrance to Atlantis to be, turn to page 22.

8

"Well, you can think whatever you want, but I was there," you tell Horton. "There's a real place called Atlantis. It still exists. It has existed for more than three thousand years, and the Atlanteans are very much alive. What's more, they're quite a bit brighter and kinder than most people who are walking around *above* the sea. You're just jealous that you weren't with me." You look at Horton defiantly.

"Okay, okay!" he replies. "Take it easy. Sure you were there. And if you have any real intention of going back, I'm going with you."

You hesitate for a moment, just long enough to make him wonder whether or not he's welcome.

"I'm not so sure I can get you in," you say. "The entrance requirements are pretty strict down there. Not every visitor is allowed in, you know. We humans don't have a very good reputation."

"What do you mean, 'we humans'? Aren't they human too?" Horton asks.

"Most certainly not," you reply. "The Atlanteans are from the planet Agyr. They left Agyr because it had fallen under the control of an Alien Elixir force called the Nodoors. The Atlanteans' time was up, and they knew it."

Go on to the next page.

Horton squirms a bit in his chair. You know that he's uncomfortable with concepts of alien forces or planets in other sectors of the galaxy. He's a scientist, and believes that if you can't see it, touch it, and analyze it, then it doesn't exist. You've almost given up trying to educate him about coexisting worlds, fifth-dimensional time and space, and equal but different life-forms. However, Horton is brave, loyal, and handy to have along in an emergency. Besides, if he returns to Atlantis with you, you'll have someone who can testify you've actually found the lost city.

"Okay, Horton," you say. "You're on. But keep an open mind, will you? It's not going to be easy. The voyage will probably be dangerous—and raising the money to set up the expedition will be difficult."

Horton flashes one of his famous smiles, leans back in his chair, opens his arms wide, and says, "A piece of cake."

Go on to the next page.

"Okay, genius. Tell me how we'll get the money and when we'll go," you reply.

"Like I said, a piece of cake. I've just gotten an International Oceanographic Grant to finance my study of whale and dolphin communication."

"You're kidding. How much?"

"Enough to get us your old research vessel, the *Maray,* and the use of a new submarine called the *Seeker II.* Good enough for you?" Horton asks.

"Let's go! I've accumulated vacation days from the lab and getting time off from classes for a research project is no problem," you reply.

Turn to page 3.

You make a run for it. You're out in the open. You might be mistaken by the Atlanteans for a Nodoor. But if you are, you'll only be stunned. You run harder, wishing you had both hands free. And you wonder why the Nodoors haven't shot you. You've almost reached the Atlanteans when you hear a *whoosh!* over your head. You ignore it—the doorway to the building is in front of you. You leap inside.

Five smiling Atlanteans greet you. One unties your arm while another turns you toward the doorway. Outside, you see the eleven Nodoors rolling around on the ground, trying to escape from what appears to be a liquid net. The more they squirm, the tighter the net grows around their bodies and weapons.

In spite of everything, you're glad to be back in Atlantis.

The End

"This is one ocean trench I didn't know about," Horton says nervously. "Is this how you found your way to Atlantis the first time?"

"No. Nothing like it. Maybe I'm—"

Before you can finish your sentence things suddenly go haywire. The *Seeker II* lurches to port and then starboard. You're thrown to the deck, bruising your arm and getting a nasty knock on your head. Horton, too, is tossed about.

"What is it? What's going on?" he shouts.

"I don't know. The controls are useless," you reply.

At that moment, everything stops. The *Seeker II* lies motionless for several minutes. Then it begins a long, slow descent. You watch the depth gauge, powerless to do anything. You're being dragged or sucked deeper into the ocean trench by an unknown force.

Turn to page 40.

While you watch, the silver capsule detaches from the creature and slides through the water toward you. A pencil-thin stream of intense red light projects from the pointed end of the capsule. The music changes pitch and volume, filling the cabin with sounds that are now approaching your threshold of pain.

Horton is captivated by the music.

"What is it? What's going on?" you shout.

The cabin of the *Seeker II* is bathed in a pinkish glow. You look at the depth gauge. You're two-thousand feet below the surface of the sea—and can't readily escape.

An eerie voice penetrates the cabin of the *Seeker II*. "Request permission to come aboard your vessel," it says.

Turn to page 17.

"You did it!" Horton yells.

"It's not over yet," you reply, wrestling with the controls. Just below you is another rocky outcropping.

"Watch out! We're going to hit this time."

Horton is right. *Thud!*

The *Seeker II* comes to a dead stop. The depth gauge reads 3,700 feet. Scanning the instruments, you note to your horror that there's a rapid loss of fuel and stored oxygen, and an increase in cabin pressure. A glance at the thermometer confirms your fear: Cabin temperature is rapidly dropping.

"The lights are dimming," Horton observes in a now calm voice. When things get really bad, Horton's bravery and calmness increase rapidly. Already he's assembling the specialized deep-diving suits for an escape from the *Seeker II*.

"Not yet, Horton," you say. "We'll hold on a bit. I've got a few tricks up my sleeve. Just wait."

Turn to page 50.

16

As commanded by the voice, you and Horton stay put inside the *Seeker II*.

"We can go to Agyr some other time," Horton says while you're waiting in the *Seeker II*. "I haven't had a chance to explore Atlantis yet. Let's find out if it's changed while you've been gone."

"The Nodoors are a dangerous group," you warn him. "It's a shame they've brought warfare here."

Moments later, you're approached by a group of Atlanteans. They lead you through an airlock into the world of Atlantis.

"Well, it looks the same as before," you whisper to Horton. "The only difference seems to be that the Atlanteans aren't smiling. They seemed so happy before."

"Warfare. It'll do it every time," replies Horton.

One of the Atlanteans guiding you is a boy about your age. He introduces himself as Marpex. "I am a transplant from Agyr," he tells you. "I have been here about six months. Atlantis is a training station for me. I am a scientist, just like the two of you. That is why I was assigned to be your guide and contact."

Turn to page 37.

Silence follows the message. The music stops. The silver capsule stops. All you can hear is your heart beating rapidly. Horton, fascinated, says, "I can't believe how beautiful that music is," as if he can still hear it. You have to do something—but what?

Your mind races. You could try to escape by making an emergency dive. Suddenly you remember that the *Seeker II* is equipped with a blaster for emergencies. You could fire that at the silver capsule.

Or, you could grant acceptance to the request to come aboard—but who or *what* is inside the silver capsule?

You wish Horton would give you a little help, but he's out of it. The decision is yours—and you have to make it quickly!

If you choose to attempt escape by making an emergency dive, turn to page 4.

If you want to use the blaster to repel or destroy the silver capsule, turn to page 62.

If you decide to let whatever is in the silver capsule board the Seeker II, *turn to page 5.*

Your transfer to the *Seeker II* is quickly accomplished, and from there you and Horton watch an unprovoked attack on the silver capsule. But, as the missile fired by the intruder cuts through the sea, the silver capsule begins to glow with a rainbow of colors. Then it fires a blue beam at the *Seeker II* and disappears from view.

Your sub shudders violently, then lifts up and rockets through the sea. As you speed across the missile's path, you see it turn—it's headed back toward the unknown vessel!

Turn to page 49.

"If that's what you want," you say to Horton, "then let's go fishing!"

"I'll monitor it for life sounds," Horton says, delighted that you've agreed to go along with him. He's already fiddling with the dials and the computer keyboard. The equipment is designed for Horton's specialty—whale and dolphin communication analysis.

"Okay," you reply, and occupy yourself with moving the *Seeker II* away from the creature ever so gently. But the creature matches your speed.

You accelerate.

It accelerates.

"Horton! What is it?" you cry. "It doesn't look like a fish or a whale. There are no fins, no gills, and no eyes."

Horton doesn't reply. He's absorbed in his work. Then he switches on the cabin speaker system and removes the listening phones from his head. An eerie music fills the *Seeker II* cabin. It's vaguely familiar. "Where's it coming from?" you ask. "The creature?"

"I'm not sure. It could be from the silver capsule attached to its side. The minute the music started, the blinking from the silver capsule stopped. See for yourself. There's just a dim glow coming from it now."

Turn to page 14.

"What do you harvest?" Horton wants to know.

"Sea plants, plankton. The fish is like a freighter. We fill him up and then he swims back to the processing plant in Atlantis. He is a major food source for us."

Horton is entranced by the concept of this giant fish harvesting food for Atlantis. He fires off question after question. Yangton and Moldoona seem delighted to answer them.

You interrupt. "I—I mean we—would like to go back with you to Atlantis. Is that possible?"

"Most certainly," Moldoona replies. "Most certainly. But our fish is only half full. We have been on cruise only a week. Would you care to come with us? If not, we could give you directions to Atlantis and radio our people to receive you. We have changed our entrance procedures since you last saw us. Evil surrounds us. Our survival is in jeopardy. The Alien Elixir forces are at work again."

You look at Horton. You know he's anxious to go on the food-gathering mission with the Atlanteans.

If you want to go straight to Atlantis, leaving Horton with Moldoona and Yangton, turn to page 45.

If you decide to join the food-gathering operation for a few days before returning to Atlantis, turn to page 57.

"That fish or whale or whatever it is, is too close for comfort," you say. "Let's get out of here."

Horton is fascinated by the beast in the murky water outside. He tries to convince you to stay a bit longer. "We don't really know where Atlantis is, do we? Let's take our time."

"My instinct and my memory both tell me to dive into that deep crack in the ocean floor," you say confidently. "We'll get to Atlantis. After all, that's what we came for. There'll be plenty of time for hunting that fish later on."

You focus all your attention on the array of dials and controls in the cramped cabin of the *Seeker II*. Your depth of 3,000 feet is enough to make decisions critical, for the pressure is intense on the hull of your craft. Any flaw in its construction, any leak in the seals around viewing ports or access hatches, could result in disaster.

Within minutes the cabin temperature begins to drop, and you and Horton pull on extra clothing. The ray from your external searchlight doesn't penetrate very far.

"Thirty-two hundred feet, three thousand three hundred twenty-five feet, three thousand four hundred seventy-five feet . . . holding steady. Echo response indicates depth to exceed nine thousand feet!" you exclaim.

Turn to page 12.

"A simple device, molecular transmission," says an Atlantean, noting your surprise and shock. "Your civilization will catch up one of these centuries."

"Departure for Agyr in eleven minutes."

You look around, surveying the Atlanteans, who have busied themselves with the usual preparation for interplanetary travel: fastening seat belts, adjusting seats to a fixed and upright position, and stowing all carry-on luggage under the seats in front of them. Then a picture appears on a large monitor at the front of the passenger cabin. You see the evacuation station and watch the final preparations for launch.

Turn to page 34.

A feeling of calmness and contentment fills you, and you sense a faint increase in pressure in the compartment. Before your eyes two human-looking figures materialize. Their bodies are bathed in a

yellowish glow that suffuses the light in the cramped compartment of the *Seeker II*.

Turn to page 30.

"You know, we Atlanteans had trouble with Earthlings when we first arrived on your planet," Grenella says. "In part, that is why we moved beneath the sea. You people are always at war. There is rarely peace on your planet."

"Maybe, but look at you," replies Horton. "You Atlanteans are at war with the Nodoors, the Alien Elixir. Your civilization can't be that much better than ours."

"To your eyes that may seem to be the case," she says with a smile. "But we Atlanteans do not attack and kill as you Earthlings do. That is why we left Agyr. The negative forces had grown too strong, too numerous for our technology to repel them without destroying them. Now our technology has advanced to a point where we can once again keep the Alien Elixir forces under control. But let us stop talking of this and begin making some plans for your stay in Agyr."

"We'd like a little excitement," you tell Grenella.

Go on to the next page.

"Well," she says, "an interesting experiment is about to take place. Volunteers are needed. I do not think it is too dangerous, but then nothing is certain. The experiment involves transmitting life-forms as musical sounds. These life-forms can affect other life-forms that listen to them. We plan to beam the music to Earth. Would you like to participate?"

"Is there another choice?" Horton ask.

"You could take part in the Universe Games as the only Earth team," Grenella replies.

If you want to participate in the musical experiment, turn to page 53.

If you decide to take part in the Universe Games, turn to page 102.

The dome house before you erupts in a brilliant orange flash. You and the Atlanteans flatten yourselves on the ground. The air clears, and before you see blackened, scorched hills. The buildings are gone.

"Not nuclear, thank heavens," says one of the Atlanteans. "It must have been a conventional weapon—a rocket left over from some Earthside war. They are nasty and they kill, but they aren't nuclear."

Before you can reply a flurry of rockets arcs through the air, heading your way. You try to run to safety, but there's no escape. The last thing you see is a group of black-and-white-clad Nodoors in the distance, laughing evilly.

Now you never will leave Atlantis.

The End

One of the figures speaks. "My name is Moldoona. I am an Atlantean, and I know about *you*." He points to you. "I was but a child when you first came to Atlantis. In your human time, that was three years ago. In our Atlantean time it was much, much longer. Welcome back."

The other figure speaks. "I am Yangton. And I, too, welcome you to Atlantis. We appreciate your acceptance of our request to board the *Seeker II*."

You are struck by the peacefulness of these two beings, but you wonder what's about to happen.

Moldoona speaks again. "We are a harvest team. Our harvester is that fish outside. See it?"

"How could we miss it?" you remark with a smile, looking out the viewing port at the giant fish.

Turn to page 21.

"Good luck, my new friend," Moldoona replies. "We will see you after the harvest."

A feeling of warmth spreads over you. It is accompanied by soft music. You feel as though you're swimming in a warm pond, while, overhead, sunlight filters through trees.

Looking down at your hands, you're shocked to see them glowing with a golden color and becoming increasingly less distinct.

"I'm vanishing!" you exclaim.

"Do not worry. You will be all right," Moldoona tells you, but his voice sounds far away and more like an echo than a real voice. Then, remembering your first welcome to Atlantis, you begin to relax. Fear drains away and is replaced by a sense of well being. You feel lighter, formless. You're glowing.

You're free.

Turn to page 38.

"It's Agyr for us," you announce.

"Hey, wait a minute! Don't I get to vote?" Horton asks.

"No time," you reply. "Let's go." You leave the *Seeker II* and breathe the refreshing air of Atlantis.

The Atlanteans greet you and escort you to the evacuation station.

"You will be met in Agyr by a guide," one tells you. "It's not safe to wander about there on your own. The Nodoors have infiltrated our society. You have to be careful."

Horton nods solemnly.

"Look at that," you exclaim, pointing at an egg-shaped, silver-colored object about the length of a football field and two stories high.

"Get aboard," you're told by a guard. Before you can question him, you and Horton are transferred from where you stand to seats in the transport vehicle—*instantaneously.*

Turn to page 23.

Moments later, you feel a slight shudder as the spacecraft rises more than nine thousand feet to the surface of the ocean and then zooms into the sky. The monitor screen reflects several surface ships below.

"What do you think they'll report they've seen?" you ask Horton. "A missile? A UFO?"

"Whatever they report," he replies, "the scientists will decide the sighting was just an optical illusion." He grins. "I know I would have—before."

During the flight, you and Horton develop a friendship with a passenger named Martullus. As the craft lands he suggests an opportunity to visit the prisons of Zuldoona where the forces hostile to Agyr have been sent to mine the rich minerals of the planet. It is off-limits to citizens of Atlantis.

You pick up negative vibrations from Martullus, but your curiosity as an explorer is strong as well. You're tantalized by this opportunity to visit a forbidden zone.

If you go with Martullus, turn to page 51.

If you decide to play it safe and check in with the Atlantean officials, turn to page 44.

"Okay, Horton, you're right," you say. "We're wasting our time. Let's get out of this coffin."

Horton nods. He finishes putting on the close-fitting inner suit and then struggles with the bulky outer suit. You have trouble with your inner suit, and panic floods your system with extra adrenaline. A pool of water appears on the floor plates of the *Seeker II*. It's the first sign of what you're sure is the ultimate disaster that awaits.

"We're sinking, Horton! Look at the depth gauge."

Horton reads if off. "Thirty-nine hundred feet, four thousand feet . . . four thousand feet steady."

"'We've got to go. It's our last chance," you say.

The water on the floor plates is now two inches deep.

At last you get your inner and outer suits on. The final step is the bulky helmet and the air tanks. Once you and Horton have them on and are breathing the air from the tanks, there's little room left in the compartment of the *Seeker II*.

Now, Horton signals with his hand.

Turn to page 108.

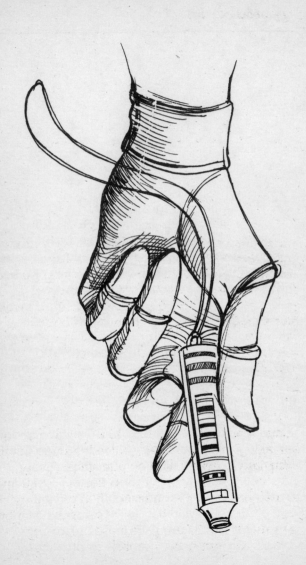

"What kind of scientist?" you ask.

"Life-form research. Humanoid, plant life, aquatic creatures."

"What are you concentrating on down here in Atlantis?" Horton asks.

"Mostly whale and dolphin research. They have great brain capacity. Most interesting. We are about to make a major breakthrough in communications with these species."

"How?" you and Horton want to know.

"We have analyzed their brain wave patterns, traced their noise waves from source to reception, and developed communicator/interpreter devices."

Marpex displays a small metallic object that he wears on a chain around his neck.

"It is simple, really. Your Earth technology is behind ours in this area, primarily because your budgets for research are mostly for weapons. Communication is the answer, not weapons."

Turn to page 47.

38

In no time at all you find yourself in the arrival chamber in Atlantis. You're surrounded by four Atlanteans, who seem to be preparing for battle, which surprises you. You know the Atlanteans are peaceful and have strong views against fighting back.

"No time to welcome your return properly," one of the Atlanteans says. "Your arrival comes at the same time as a violent attack by the Nodoors. They are only one hundred yards away. We can try to get you to headquarters, which is relatively safe, or you can join us in warding off the Nodoor attack."

If you decide to go to headquarters,
turn to page 69.

If you decide to help repel the Nodoors,
turn to page 42.

"What now?" Horton asks.

"Be patient. I'll think of something," you reply. "I should have trusted my instincts. I thought Martullus might be a Nodoor. The Nodoors look just like the Atlanteans. This is my fault."

"Enough talk! Get to work!" shouts a guard.

In all your dreams of returning to Atlantis, you never imagined ending up like this. Silently, you pick up a tool. Your life of slave labor has begun.

The End

For forty-three minutes, the *Seeker II* is pulled deeper and deeper into the trench.

"Depth eighty-six hundred feet," you report.

"Hey, it's getting lighter outside. Look!" Horton says, peering through one of the viewing ports.

Sure enough, an area directly below you is much lighter. You can see the shadow of the *Seeker II*!

Deeper yet. At 9,100 feet, you break into what looks like sunlight. Yet you're still surrounded by water.

The *Seeker II* shudders to a halt. A clear bubble encircles it. With a *whoosh,* the sea water is sucked out of the bubble. And the *Seeker II* bumps gently to the bubble's floor.

"Now what?" Horton asks.

A soft voice answers for you. "Welcome to Atlantis. This is a transit station. We are currently under attack by the Nodoors." You wonder why the voice is giving you so much information, but you don't say anything, and it continues. "There is no immediate danger to Atlantis, but as a precaution we are ferrying some of our people back to the home planet Agyr."

"I thought Agyr was hostile territory to you Atlanteans. Isn't that why you left?" you ask.

Go on to the next page.

"Quite right. But things are better now in Agyr. Forgive me, but there isn't much time for talk. We monitored you from the beginning of your undersea journey. Welcome back to Atlantis."

You look at Horton with surprise and amazement. "They remember me!" you exclaim.

"Big deal. It was only three years ago," he replies.

Once again, the soothing voice speaks. "If you want to go to Agyr where it is safer, leave your vessel, and you will be transported to the evacuation station. If not, stay where you are for the time being."

If you decide to go to Agyr, turn to page 32.

If you decide to stay in Atlantis, turn to page 16.

"I'll help you ward off the Nodoors," you announce. You're excited, but fearful that this decision could be your last.

"Fine. We need all the help we can get," the Atlantean tells you. "The Nodoors have secured new weapons. We think they got them from arms dealers in your world. They are crude weapons, but nevertheless they kill."

Slowly but surely your body is beginning to reform. The four Atlanteans around you are handsome people, a few years older than you. They're dressed in standard Atlantean clothes—jumpsuits made of a light but tough fabric, not found above the sea. They're softspoken and appear kindly.

Go on to the next page.

"Here. Take this, but use it sparingly," says one of the Atlanteans. "It will stun your opponent without killing, but its effectiveness increases with each stunning. It can be dangerous because ultimately it will cause biological changes."

You examine the stun weapon, a harmless-looking plastic device much like a remote TV channel changer.

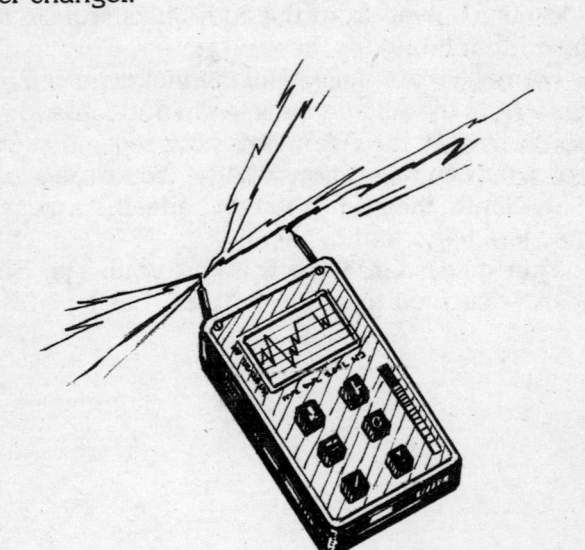

Turn to page 67.

44

"No thanks, Martullus," you say. "We'd love to go, but we'll check in here first." You and Horton head for several uniformed officials, in search of the guide you were promised.

Martullus looks worried and hastily moves away, saying that he will be in touch with you later on. Watching his hasty departure, you're convinced that he had something to hide from you and maybe even from the authorities. You're relieved that he's gone.

Formalities are quick, and the welcome you receive from the Atlanteans is warm and reassuring. You learn that the Atlanteans have regained control of the central portions of Agyr. You're also told that Atlantis, their Earth station beneath the sea, is now less important to them.

Your guide, Grenella, is about your age. She seems delighted to talk with "real" Earth people.

Turn to page 26.

"I'm anxious to see Atlantis again," you say. "I'd like to go now. Okay with you, Horton?"

"Sure. I'm happy here," Horton replies. "Atlantis will be there when we finish the harvest. Go ahead."

Moldoona gives a series of rapid-fire orders to the ship's computer. You are startled by what you think you hear—a laugh coming from the computer! Moldoona chuckles also.

"We are set to arrange transport for you to Atlantis," he tells you a few moments later. "You will be met in an arrival chamber."

A surge of excitement and wonder fills you. Atlantis is a world so like and yet so different from your world. You remember it's special quality—the quality that tempted you to give up your life on the surface.

During your first visit to Atlantis, you seriously considered never leaving. The peacefulness, the evenness, the joy of Atlantean life made you feel that it was better than the life you knew. Except for the Nodoors.

Turn to page 59.

"I never did believe in running from a fight," you say. "Let's see who the intruder is. Are we armed?" you ask.

"Definitely, except that we Atlanteans do not believe in attack. Hostility begets hostility, you know," Moldoona replies.

"So what can we do to defend ourselves?"

"We have energy deflectors that simply return whatever is directed at us. They are very effective—most of the time."

Looking out the viewing port, you think you can see the outline of the intruder vessel in the ink-black water.

"We just deploy a solution that enhances energy deflections," Moldoona says, as the computer organizes the release of a substance that clouds the water around the capsule.

"What will happen to the *Seeker II?*" you ask.

"That I can't answer."

Before the substance totally clouds the area, you get a glimpse of the intruder.

"It's a sub. It's a conventional missle-bearing attack sub, an Earth craft!" you cry. "It's not Nodoors!"

Turn to page 111.

"Easy for you to say, but look at you and the Nodoors," you point out. "Why don't you communicate with them?"

"No one is perfect," Marpex replies.

"Well, let's try to communicate," you say.

"If you wish. I *was* planning to show you some rather interesting whale and dolphin research. But we can observe a group of Nodoors who are approaching us with a peace proposal, instead. It is your choice." Marpex waits for your response.

If you decide to go to the whale and dolphin research area, turn to page 84.

If you decide to go to the peace talks, turn to page 60.

Before you realize how it has happened, you're on the light beam, traveling back to Agyr.

"The experiment was a success," the director of the Sight and Sound Research Group says. "We'll have to do it again, but longer next time and to more people."

On Earth, meanwhile, news of the music of the spheres has spread. There is talk that the music is a sign of peace, a sign of love, a sign of the end of the bad times, the end of war and greed.

The End

"Look!" Horton shouts suddenly. "The giant fish. It's coming with us." The fish is keeping pace with your now supersonic sub.

Soon you, Horton, and the giant fish emerge into sunlight and a calm sea, far from where the attack occurred.

The giant fish nudges the *Seeker II* once or twice with its sucker-like snout, as if saying good-bye, and sinks back under the sea.

"Kind of like a guide and a protector, don't you think?" asks Horton.

You nod your head, once more in awe of the Atlanteans. Then you offer up a kind of prayer to Moldoona and Yangton and Atlantis.

"We'll go back, Horton. I promise," you say.

The End

"If we wait too long all we'll be is a memory for our friends. I say we have a better chance if we bail out now," Horton says firmly.

Meanwhile, you've desperately been trying to activate the emergency power systems. The pressure at 3,700 feet is well beyond the maximum depth capacity of the special suits.

Beads of sweat break out on your forehead, even though the temperature in the *Seeker II* has now dropped to 42 degrees Fahrenheit. Horton finishes assembling the deep-diving suits and begins to get into his. The bitter taste of fear fills your mouth as you stand frozen in the semidarkness.

"Come on!" Horton shouts, thrusting your deep-dive suit at you.

The emergency power indicator shows the beginning of power gain, but it's slow in coming up to full power. You glance at Horton, weighing your options.

If you decide to go with Horton in the deep-dive suits, turn to page 35.

If you choose to remain in the Seeker II and keep trying for emergency power, turn to page 109.

"Follow me, don't ask questions, and do not look too inquisitive," Martullus tells you. "Pretend you are on a fact-finding mission from another planet. We get them all the time in Agyr now that it's been reconquered by us." Martullus walks purposefully away.

You and Horton follow. It's hard not to stare at the world around you. It's entirely different from Earth and Atlantis: there are no actual buildings, only crystalline structures that seem to revolve in response to the planetary movement around the suns of Agyr.

Other living areas seem to be gaseous modules that expand or contract as needed. The living forms inside these gaseous blobs remind you of cell structure.

The light in Agyr is provided by three suns and is diffused in crystals, probably to break up harmful radiation. It gives the effect of being in a kaleidoscope.

There is no traffic: no cars, no transporters, no air scooters. You mention this to Martullus.

"We have no need of external vehicles to travel short distances," he tells you. "Our brains are our vehicles. We need only wish and desire to be transported from one place to another."

Turn to page 86.

52

The beetles turn away from the controls of the transporter to look at you. They seem to be laughing, but you can't tell because their faces are stiff. Only their eyes reflect their feelings.

You and Horton are hurried off the transporter. Outside in the sweet-smelling air, you're surrounded by a group of people in orange uniforms. They carry primitive weapons, mostly swords. And one is carrying two ankle chains.

"Over here, worms, over here," he shouts.

Before you can resist, the ankle chains are clamped on, and you and Horton are led away to the prison farms of Zuldoona. You can only hope that you will be freed by Atlantean forces.

It gets hot, and the wind picks up as you and Horton begin work in the machine shops of the farm.

Turn to page 39.

"Music! Turned into music!" you exclaim. "Let's give it a try, Horton. How long will the experiment last?" you ask Grenella.

"Oh, it will be brief. Earthlings cannot take much change. Any major change really upsets them, you know."

"Okay. Let's go!" you say. Horton nods in agreement.

It doesn't take long to get to the laboratory of the Sight and Sound Research Group. You're accepted as volunteers for the experiment without too much questioning. Not many others have volunteered for this opportunity.

Go on to the next page.

You, Horton, and Grenella are placed in a small, brightly lit, soundproof room. You notice a rapid increase in temperature. Before you can say anything or change your mind, you realize that you're

traveling as sound carried by light waves. You no longer have any body sensations.

Go on to the next page.

56

The beam of light is a comfortable way to cross space, and before long, you see the shape of Earth with its halo of clouds. You experience a rushing sensation and a feeling of being squeezed as you enter Earth's atmosphere and gravitational field.

Turn to page 103.

"We'd better not get separated," you tell Horton. "Let's go along and see how this fish performs." You turn to Moldoona. "Do we come with you in the capsule, or do we follow you in the *Seeker II*?" you ask.

"Come with us. But should you not communicate with your surface ship?" Moldoona asks. "We do not want them to worry. They might start an underwater search for you. And that could be embarrassing for Atlantis."

"Don't worry. The *Seeker II* is equipped for sustained underwater travel. We have enough food and air and fuel for up to three weeks. The crew of the *Maray* knows we might break contact. But, anyway, I'll set the transmitter of the *Seeker II* to give a periodic 'all's well' signal topside. Let's go."

In almost no time, the four of you are aboard the silver capsule, transported to it by a dematerializer, part of the Atlantean technology. The inside of the capsule is uncluttered by instruments, except for one medium-sized display screen that responds to information requests given orally. There are several comfortable seats and a number of viewing ports from which the works of the giant fish can be seen.

You're about to ask a question, when a gentle voice comes over the capsule speaker.

Turn to page 74.

58

You're barely aware of being lifted up and carried away. The voices you think you hear are saying, "Be . . . careful . . . with this . . . one."

Maybe they're talking about you, maybe not. You don't really care. You drift off into a dreamlike state that is comforting and pleasant.

Then you feel pain. It's followed by music—the same music you heard aboard the *Seeker II*.

Slowly and with apprehension, you swim up through the darkness and confusion until you break into full consciousness.

"Welcome back to Atlantis," are the first words you hear.

The End

The Nodoors are as different from the Atlanteans as night is from day. They're suspicious, greedy, untrustworthy, and warlike. They take every opportunity to upset, interrupt, and even destroy Atlantean life.

During that first visit, you had begun to learn that life was a balance between the extremes of good and bad, light and dark. But you had difficulty in fully accepting this thought. The Atlanteans themselves never worried much about the Nodoors. They accepted the existence of the negative and the positive.

"The more you fight them, the more they will attack," said your Atlantean friends. "To succeed is to work from your strength, not to combat their strength."

You didn't really understand what they meant. But you remember that your experiences in Atlantis were all positive when you dealt with Atlanteans fairly and openly.

"I'm ready, Moldoona," you say.

Turn to page 31.

60

"I'm interested in the Nodoors," you tell Marpex. "My last experience with them was not good, but there's always hope for change. Let me go to the peace talks as an observer."

"Fine. I could use an objective opinion. We keep having these peace meetings, but they always break down just when we think we are getting somewhere."

The trip to the neutral zone where the meetings are to be held doesn't take long. You're ushered into a building that resembles a Greek temple.

A messenger rushes up to Marpex and tells him that he's needed in the control room to consult on communication problems. Horton decides to accompany him. You're on your own.

Tall, fluted columns surround an inner courtyard. The roof of the building is missing, destroyed decades before in one of the Nodoor attacks.

The courtyard is crowded with Atlanteans and Nodoors. In the center of the courtyard, around a table made of something that looks like white gold, sit the leaders of both sides. They wear blue robes. You overhear an Atlantean explaining that the color symbolizes coming together for negotiation. Among the leaders, you can't tell a Nodoor from an Atlantean.

Turn to page 75.

"We'll try the blaster, Horton," you exclaim. "Just one quick shot off their port bow as a warning. That should do it."

"I don't know. Every action has an equal and opposite reaction. You blast, they may blast right back. I don't see any reason for force right now. But you're the ship commander, so be my guest. Blast away."

You enter a series of commands into the computer that controls the laser-operated blast device.

The display indicates *Blaster Operational*.

Outside the *Seeker II* the silver capsule hovers in an almost ominous calm—quiet, controlled, persistent.

The voice repeats its request. "Permission to come aboard. Requesting permission to come aboard."

Your hand moves slowly toward the Fire button.

Turn to page 66.

"Since we're staying, is there anything we can do to help?" you ask.

Moldoona shakes his head no. "This could be most unpleasant," he warns you. "The Nodoors are in constant battle with us. They are not afraid to use force." Moldoona busies himself with a control pod that has silently appeared next to his seat.

Yangton, meanwhile, has disappeared to the aft portion of the capsule to ready emergency gear to deal with the intruder.

Once again, the computer voice floods the compartment. The tone this time is more elevated, slightly more excited. "Commander, the intruder is closing in. Its weapons system is armed. Our escape routes are being compromised."

"Yes. Yes. I know. I have eyes, too," Moldoona answers impatiently.

"Do not be angry, Commander. I am only mechanical and doing my job. But I do not want to be destroyed."

"All right, all right. Remain cool. I am sorry," Moldoona replies.

"Your apology is accepted, Commander, but we had better act quickly."

Turn to page 99.

64

"Let's get out of here," you say. "The sea is loaded with subs: Russian, U.S., and who knows what else. They play for keeps and they're armed to the teeth. A mistake could be gravely dangerous."

"I hear you," Moldoona replies. "Prepare for descent to Atlantis."

"Yes, sir, Commander," says the computer.

Noiselessly, the silver capsule accelerates at a downward angle, diving to the ocean floor. You expect enemy fire at any moment, but none follows. Eleven minutes later, the dive finished, the capsule scoots along the silent ocean floor.

You and Horton are glued to the viewing ports, watching the underwater world slip by. Strange fish, tangled plants, a jumble of rocks. Suddenly you see a deep crack in the ocean floor.

"Here we are," says Moldoona.

"That was easy," you say.

"These rapid descents are dangerous but effective," Moldoona replies. Then, "Prepare for recovery," he orders the computer.

Turn to page 113.

66

You press the button, and there's a barely perceptible flash of light as the blaster emits a laser beam.

The beam creates a tunnel through the water off the port side of the silver capsule. Your finger is ready on the button for a second blast. The computer targeting device centers on the silver capsule. You activate the radio broadcast system for external communication purposes.

"Permission denied. Identify yourself, or the next blast will be aimed directly at you."

You dredge up a memory of a similar situation—a vision of blasting and of the blast being returned with a violence many times greater than your blast. The vision turns into pictures of roselike blooms forming, reforming in darkness that envelops you.

Turn to page 107.

Cautiously, your group moves outside the arrival building into the beautiful undersea world. Atlantis is in the form of an enormous dome, complete with a sun source—reflectors of sunlight on top of the ocean. Flowers, trees, and fields stretch across a rolling terrain. Clear, dome houses like little bubbles dot the landscape. You even see clouds on the horizon.

"Where to?" you ask in a whisper.

"Over to that dome. It is a good spot from which to survey the area because it is on a small hill. The Nodoors are obvious in their black and white uniforms. We will watch them from there."

Preparing to repel an enemy in the midst of so much beauty and peacefulness seems unreal to you. The fields are well tended, the gardens are full and healthy. No one except the members of your group is to be seen.

"Watch out!" someone yells.

Turn to page 28.

68

"Heavens no! I'm not an Earth creature, as you call those misguided souls who live above the sea. I'm a renegade," you exclaim.

The Nodoor examines your face closely and then turns to talk with the others in his band. They're a tough-looking group, heavily armed with an assortment of weapons of the type most often found with above-sea armies. You try to look casual, at ease, but you're scared out of your wits.

"Renegade, huh! Renegade from what to what?" the Nodoor asks, frowning.

"Can't stand being an Atlantean. I want some real action. I want to go over to the Nodoors," you reply.

"If you're lying, it will mean your life," the Nodoor replies. "Understand?"

"I do."

"Okay, let's go. And no funny business from you."

Two Nodoors stay as close to you as possible as the group moves quickly through the country. You're headed toward Atlantia, the metropolis of Atlantis.

Turn to page 85.

"I won't be much help to you here," you tell the Atlantean. "Let me go to headquarters. Maybe I can be useful. I could try to get in touch with some of the Nodoors I knew when I was last in Atlantis."

"Getting there may be dangerous. You will have to cross territory that's now held by Nodoors. Here, I will show you the way."

The Atlantean produces a map on a hand-held computer screen. The route seems simple enough to follow—and if you're lucky you won't meet any Nodoors.

"Good luck!" you say. "I'll see you later on." You slip out of the arrival building and head for a dense grove of trees about four hundred yards away. You check the stun device the Atlanteans have given you. They explained that it will not kill, but that with repeated use it becomes very dangerous.

Running doubled over, close to the ground, you reach the woods safely. There's no sign of the Nodoors. You're now hidden from view.

Go on to the next page.

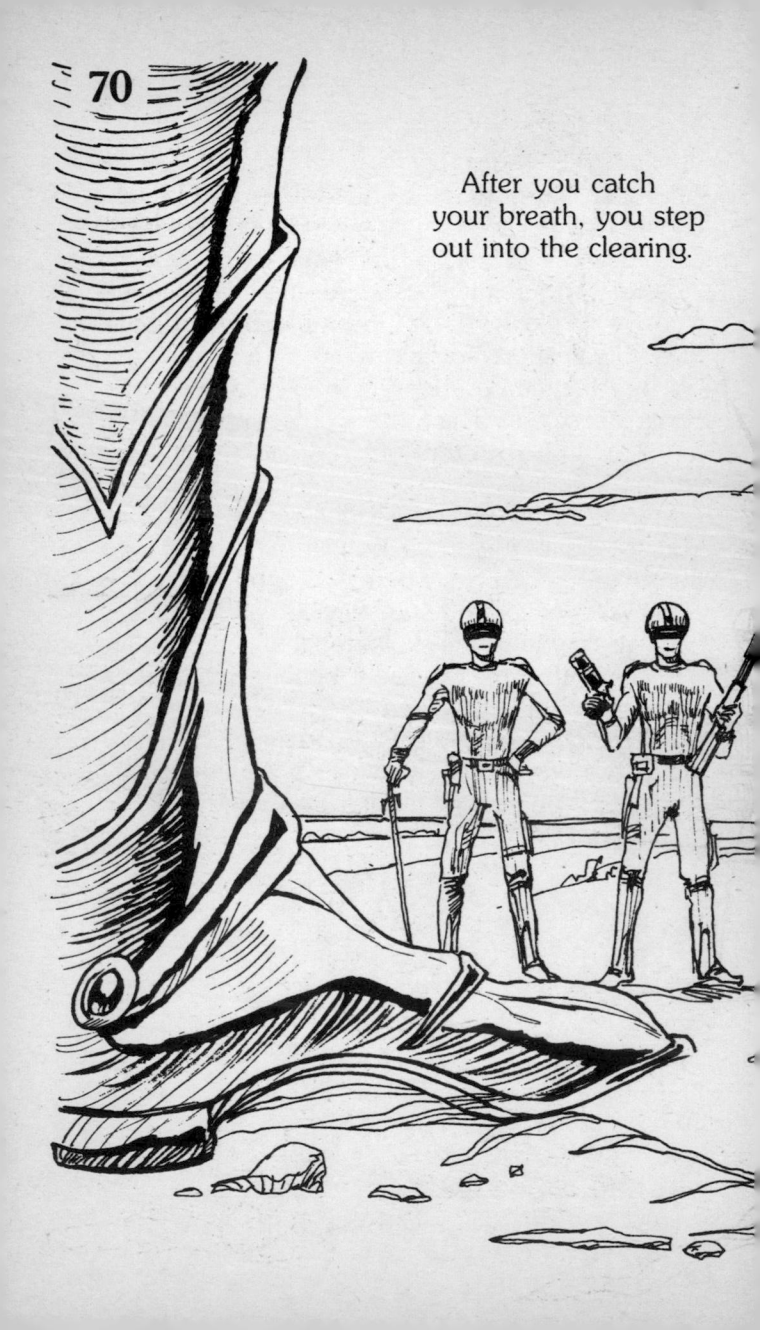

After you catch
your breath, you step
out into the clearing.

Suddenly you're surrounded by eleven Nodoors.

Go on to the next page.

"Hands up! Don't move!" one cries. "You're dressed oddly for an Atlantean. Wait a minute. Are you an Earth creature? An above-sea person?"

You pause for only the briefest moment.

If you invent a story about being a renegade Atlantean, turn to page 68.

If you admit that you're an Earthling, turn to page 79.

You have some trouble adjusting the artificial gills, but finally they feel fairly comfortable, and you leave with Marpex through the southeast port. Horton, much to his disappointment, remains in Altantis to monitor your actions on a three-dimensional TV by picking up signals from both you and Marpex. The signals originate from broadcast devices in the artificial gill pieces.

You rise several thousand feet to the zone in which whales can function.

"Where is he?" you want to know.

"Who?" Marpex replies.

"The whale."

"I'm right here," says a voice.

Startled, you look over your shoulder and see an immense shadow—the outline of a humpback whale. A whale has spoken, and you—the first human ever to do so—understood him!

"Is this the one?" the whale asks.

"Yes. He's your hostage," Marpex replies.

"Good. Take hold of this. It's an old whaler's harpoon line. I'll swim, and you hold tight."

"Wait a minute. When do I get to go back?" you ask, still slightly amazed that you're communicating with a whale.

"When we're satisfied that the Atlanteans don't intend to harm us," replies the whale. With that, he gives an enormous push with his tail, and you're suddenly pulled through the water at astonishing speed.

Turn to page 95.

"Be advised that we are being surveyed and approached by an unknown vessel," says the voice.

Moldoona sits up straight and and glances at Yangton.

"Vessel is armed with primitive, but lethal, atomic warheads," the voice continues.

Moldoona asks calmly, "Do you know if any of your Navy's ships are on patrol here? Would they be searching for you?"

"Never can tell," you reply. "The Navy is all over the place."

Moldoona speaks to the ship's computer-controlled system. "Prepare for possible enemy activity. Deploy confusion gear. Set energy deflection shields."

The silver capsule detaches from the side of the giant fish, and descends 500 feet. An inky substance flows into the water, creating a cloud around the capsule.

"If you wish to return to the *Seeker II*," Moldoona says to you, "please do so. We must prepare for hostile action. The intruders could either be Earth people or our arch enemies, the Nodoors of the Alien Elixir."

If you choose to return to the Seeker II,
turn to page 19.

*If you stay aboard the Atlantean capsule,
turn to page 63.*

As you move through the crowd, you overhear another snatch of conversation, spoken by a man leaning furtively toward a woman. Both are dressed in Atlantean clothes.

"They will never suspect. We can get them all. Set the time for—"

You don't hear the time because a shout goes up in the courtyard. The two people you overheard are moving toward the rear of the hall.

If you follow them, turn to page 78.

If you try to warn those around you, turn to page 104.

"Follow me," the voice says again. You follow and are led on an easy journey from the horror of the beetles to the security of the Atlantean Council Headquarters. There you're honored as a guest and as a two-time visitor to the world of Atlantis. You feel proud. But you're sad as well. You wish that Horton were there to share the Atlanteans' honor—you wish Horton were anywhere.

The End

78

The crowd is thick, and moving through the corridors surrounding the courtyard is difficult. As you push through the crowd, you learn that the shouting was about a Nodoor complaint. They wanted a round table instead of a square one for negotiating. The Atlanteans accepted, and the change is now being made.

"Where are they?" you ask yourself out loud.

"Who?" comes a response from a boy your own age, dressed in Nodoor clothes.

"Two Atlanteans. Or, at least, they were dressed like Atlanteans. I think they're planning to set off a bomb to ruin the peace talks," you reply.

"Follow me," the boy says. "I know a way around this crowd."

You skirt the crowd quickly and, to your relief, catch up with the two you overheard. They're huddled over a box.

Turn to page 88.

"Yes, I'm from above the sea, an Earth creature as you say. I'm not involved in your fight, and I don't want to be."

"Then why are you here and what are you doing in our world?"

"I'm here because of an accident aboard my research sub. By sheer chance I was lucky enough to make it safely into your world. I don't know how, and I can only say I'd be dead if I weren't here."

The Nodoors talk quietly for several minutes, trying to decide what to do with you.

Zap!

An enormous electric shock overwhelms all of you. You're stunned and slump to the ground, unable to move or speak. Your eyes focus on distant objects, your heart flutters, your muscles twitch. Sounds reaching you are like noises in a long tunnel. They echo and reverberate, making little or no sense to you.

Time ticks by, and it, too, seems unfamiliar. Your body feels as if it's made of rubber.

Turn to page 58.

80

The audience seems frightened at first. They look at the stage, but the musicians have stopped playing. Your music swells and reverberates in the broad canyon surrounded by rolling California hills.

The people lose their fear. And as they relax, the music you've brought from Agyr fills them with a sense of joy and hope.

"Our time is up. We have to go back," Grenella says. "Will you stay with us and help with these experiments?"

"Yes, certainly," you reply.

Turn to page 48.

"The secret is that Earth is a chosen planet," one Atlantean tells you. "A planet for experiments by the Universe Committee. Life-forms are given more chances on Earth than in any other place in the universe. But the Universe Committee is worried. The life-form experiments are not going well. The committee is thinking of ending the experiment—soon. We Atlanteans are preparing to head back to Agyr."

"How much time do we have?" you ask.

"It depends on events on Earth, but the word around Agyr is a year or two at most."

"What about us?" you ask.

"Come with us, if you wish, but if you do there can be no turning back," he replies.

You can't answer for Horton, but Atlantis has just become *your* chosen world.

The End

"Police! Police! Help!" you yell, pushing through what you think is the exit in the gaseous blob. You and Horton reach an external corridor. Facing you are the two energy forms, which now turn into enormous beetles. Their ferocious faces are smooth, shiny, and fiery red. Sharp tusks spiral upward from their mandibles. They move toward you, blocking your path.

"Save yourself, Horton!" you cry.

"There is no escape." The thin, spiky voice comes from one of the beetles.

You twist away and dart to one side. A sticky fluid splashes over your back. One of your arms becomes glued to your side. You turn and squirm and manage to run off.

Another shot of the fluid catches you in the middle of the back, but you keep going.

You hear a frightening, agonized cry, followed by a horrific crunching sound. You glance back. Horton is in the jaws of one of the beetles. The other beetle is still after you.

Turn to page 98.

As Marpex guides you and Horton to the research area, he talks about the progress the Atlanteans have made in communicating with whales and dolphins.

"We have made contact with a group of humpback whales as well," Marpex says. "They are quite wary of us. I think they feel that we are trying to lure them into a 'kill zone.' Their experience with humanoid life-forms has not been good, as you know," he adds.

"Tell them that you don't want to hurt them," you suggest.

"Oh, we have," he replies. "They want us to show good faith by offering a hostage. Any volunteers?"

If you volunteer to be a hostage,
turn to page 93.

If you decide not to be a hostage,
turn to page 105.

You know that the Nodoors don't really believe you, and you keep an eye out for an opportunity to escape. Fighting rages from house to house in the beautiful city of Atlantia. Destruction is widespread, and you grieve for the Atlantean people.

As a security measure, the Nodoors stop to tie one of your arms to your side. They also take your stun device. Having one arm tied doesn't slow you down, but it certainly limits your ability to escape.

"Over there! Look! Five Atlanteans in that building! Get them," yells the Nodoor leader.

This is your chance, maybe your only chance.

Turn to page 11.

86

The inhabitants of Agyr are Earthlike—when you look at them directly. But if you turn your concentration away from them for as much as a second, they quickly become almost protoplasmic. Or maybe they're sheer energy, pulsing and vibrating.

At one point, you glimpse yourself in some reflected light from a crystalline structure, and you're shocked and horrified to see no human characteristics, only energy! But before fear takes over, a feeling of knowledge and well-being spreads through you, allowing you to accept your non-Earth form.

Martullus slips into a gaseous blob, which immediately expands to hold the three of you.

"Stay put!" he commands. "Keep quiet."

You look outside the gaseous blob, and see the pulsing shapes of three uniformed Atlanteans who seem to be conducting a blob-to-blob search. This could be trouble, you think. Maybe you should give up the plan to visit Zuldoona and report in to these uniformed Atlanteans. After all, you were supposed to be given a guide when you arrived on Agyr.

If you choose to leave the gaseous nodule and report in to the Atlanteans, turn to page 110.

If you decide to stay put, turn to page 90.

"Horton! Look!" you exclaim.

"I don't believe it," he says.

Below you, in what, moments before, was a jumble of rocks, now lies a glowing, shining white tunnel three times the size of a football field.

Once again, the eerie music fills the *Seeker II* as you're pulled into the tunnel of light. You experience no fear, no hesitation, only joy at finally returning to Atlantis.

The End

You lunge forward, throwing yourself on the two huddled figures.

There is a gigantic flash of white light as a miniaturized neutron weapon explodes, disintegrating everything within two miles.

Your surface research ship, the *Maray*, records a minor earthquake on its monitoring devices. Gaseous bubbles rise to the surface.

The End

"What are they looking for?" you ask, peering through the blob at the uniformed Atlanteans.

"Quiet!" Martullus commands again. "Don't move!"

"What's happening?" you whisper.

"Police!"

The three of you freeze. Outside, the officers scrutinize the gaseous blob and then move on very slowly, occasionally looking back.

"I fixed them," Martullus brags after they're gone.

"How?" you ask.

"Simple energy block. It interrupts their thought processes and screws up their analyzers. Easy when you know how."

"Have you done this often? I mean, have you escaped from the police often?" you ask.

"Many times, my young friends. Many times," he replies.

Once again, that feeling of foreboding passes over you. Something about Martullus is very disturbing.

Go on to the next page.

"Now, out we go. I have managed an escort to Zuldoona. For long-range trips, we do need transport. And ours has just arrived." Outside, you can just make out a torpedo-shaped blue plastic vehicle. Two energy forms wait beside it.

"Come on, let's go," says Martullus. "We cannot waste time."

You hesitate. You still want to visit the forbidden zone, but you're not sure you want to go there with Martullus.

If you decide to make a dash for the police, who are still barely in view, turn to page 82.

If you follow Martullus's commands, turn to page 96.

"What were you doing with Martullus?" the Atlantean officer demands.

"Oh, nothing, really," you reply.

"Where did you meet him, and where were you going?" he asks.

Horton pushes you aside. "Officer, we were headed with Martullus to Zuldoona. We're scientists from Earth and we mean no harm."

"Oh, dear, you stupid Earthlings. Martullus is a slaver. He probably offered you a tour of Zuldoona. Some tour. You would have spent the rest of your life in those prison camps. They are not Atlantean, you know. They are in the Zone of Determinus, the zone to which negative energy is banished."

"What now?" you ask.

"We will transport you back to Earth,"—the Atlantean smiles—"where you belong."

The End

"Me!" you answer with a grin. "The whales are probably smart enough to know that hurting me won't get them anywhere. What do I do?"

"You go with me to meet one of the whales outside the southeast entrance port to Atlantis. He will take you with him to a group of whales that will hold you hostage until our talks are over."

"How will I breathe?" you ask.

Marpex smiles and walks over to a cabinet. You're surprised when he returns and hands you a small device, much like a pair of stereo headphones. "Use these," he says. "They are artificial gills. They will enable you to survive at extreme depths." He then picks up a laser scalpel. "But first . . ." With no pain to you, Marpex makes two small slits in your neck and plugs in the artificial gills.

"Now you are all set for one of the most amazing journeys of your life."

Turn to page 73.

Less than thirty minutes later, you arrive at the algae-covered hull of a sunken ocean liner. Its outlines are mysterious and foreboding in the shadowy depths.

"You'll stay here for now," the whale says, propelling you toward the ship with a flip of his large tail.

For the next two days, you remain isolated in the old first-class lounge of the sunken ship. You wait and wait, hoping that things will go well between the whales and the Atlanteans.

Your guards, young whales and dolphins, are friendly and kind, but time hangs heavy, and fear permeates your thoughts.

Then without warning, you're summoned from your ghostly prison and returned to Marpex and Atlantis.

Turn to page 112.

96

You and Horton leave the gaseous blob and climb into the transport vehicle.

"Look!" Horton says in a horrified whisper. He points at the two creatures up front.

As you look at them, they change from their energy states into red beetles.

Martullus climbs in behind you, nods to the beetles, and the transporter accelerates. It soon reaches its cruising speed and arcs out over the horizon. Below, you see the crumpled hills of Agyr, the frozen seas, the deserts of glass, and the petrified forests. Volcanoes appear in great clusters.

Finally, you come to a craterlike area, remote and beautiful. The center of the crater is a lake of brilliant yellow fluid. Around its shores spread orchards and fields. Everything about the place looks like a farming valley—productive, well-run, and successful.

"Welcome to Zuldoona," Martullus says with a chuckle. "You will like it here."

Turn to page 52.

You look—and see life-forms, many of them quite strange, taking up positions on the squares.

In a flash of recognition you exclaim, "Why, it's like a giant chess game!"

"You are right," Grenella says. "It is not exactly chess, but that is close enough. The elimination rounds are going on right now. I will explain the rules, and you and Horton will play as Earth. Your first opponent can be Venus. Good luck!"

Horton is an ace chess player, and you're not so bad yourself, but something is worrying you.

"What happens if we lose?" you say out loud, fearing death to the losers.

Grenella laughs.

"Oh, you Earthlings. Everything is good or bad, black or white, to you down there. Enjoy the game. Play it. There is no prize for winning and no penalty for losing."

"Very strange indeed," you reply.

But Horton has already developed an opening strategy. "Let's play," he shouts.

The End

With a desperate lunge, you squeeze into a tiny, green, gaseous blob. Instantly it expands to accommodate you. The beetle stops outside the blob, either uncertain about where you are, or unable to enter the blob. You slump down, trying to remain calm, but Horton's horrible end is etched on your mind. It's all your fault, you think.

"Follow me," a gentle voice says. Looking up, you see a form materializing in front of you. It's humanoid. You feel no fear.

Turn to page 77.

Yangton suddenly reappears from the aft section.

"I have ordered Herman to exit the area," he reports.

You're about to ask who Herman is, when you see the giant fish swim away with massive sweeps of its tail. The silver capsule rocks to the movement of the water.

"If you wish to dive for Atlantis and safety, we'll do it, and leave this intruder. We have time to accomplish this," Moldoona tells you and Horton.

"What's the alternative?" you ask.

"The alternative is to stay here and repel the intruder," he replies.

If you want a rapid escape to Atlantis,
turn to page 64.

If you choose to stay and ward off the intruder,
turn to page 46.

No sooner are you out of the *Seeker II* than you're picked up by a glasslike sphere. The seawater slowly drains out of the sphere and is replaced with a gaseous substance. A moment later the music you heard earlier fills your ears. You wonder how you can hear it through your dive helmet, then you stop wondering and just listen. The music is soft and soothing. Suddenly a voice cuts in over the music. "Be not afraid," it says. "An Atlantean research team has recovered you. You may remove your dive helmets if you wish. The sphere has been filled with a breathable gas, similar to oxygen. Relax. We will return to our base. You will enjoy your stay in Atlantis."

Outside the sphere, you see the giant fishlike shape. It pulses and turns as a cable attaches your sphere to the silver capsule on its side.

The End

"On to the Games!" you cry, picturing yourself wearing the gold medal—or perhaps the laurel wreath—of an Olympic victor.

"Wait a minute," Horton protests. "What do we do? I mean we're marine biologists, not athletes."

"Don't worry. We'll find something," you reply.

Grenella leads the way to an area outside the main living section of the city. It's a field criss-crossed with lines joining green and white squares. On the perimeter of this patchwork field are tents of brightly colored fabric. Above the tents are flags and pennants representing parts of the universe you never even knew existed.

"You can use this tent," Grenella says, leading you to a box-shaped tent of brilliant red. Horton busies himself making a pennant symbolizing Earth. He hoists it on a flagpole outside the tent.

"What now, Grenella?" you ask.

"Look at the field," she replies. "What do you see?"

Turn to page 97.

You're now free-floating musical sounds. You bump into Earth sound waves and television waves and light radiation waves. These waves cause some distortion in your sound-wave pattern, but the experiment controller back in Agyr succeeds in keeping your pattern clear.

"Horton, let's invade the sound of a rock concert!" you suggest excitedly. "We'll change the music. We'll give them something they'll never forget."

"Great! Let's do it. How about you, Grenella?"

"Count me in," Grenella replies.

You select a concert going on in an outdoor arena in California, just outside of Los Angeles. Ninety-seven thousand people are sprawled on the ground listening to a group that is famous for hard ryhthm.

"Now," you shout.

You, Horton, and Grenella block the rock band and replace their sound with your life music.

Softness. Harmony. Music of the spheres flows over the crowd.

Turn to page 80.

"Stop those two!" you say to the Atlanteans and Nodoors nearest you. "I think they're going to set off a bomb!"

No one believes you. You're quickly removed from the building and taken into protective custody by the Atlantean security forces, who think you're crazy.

Moments later, you're blinded by a flash of white light from an explosion. It's the last thing you remember in your humanoid form.

The End

"No volunteering for me—it's too risky," you say to Marpex. "I'm for staying here."

"I do not blame you," he replies. "How about you, Horton?"

"I'll go. It's an opportunity not to be missed."

Horton puts on some artificial-gill equipment which will allow him to breathe underwater, and soon departs with Marpex. At the same time, two Atlantean technicians join you to help monitor Horton's progress and Marpex's talks with the whales. You settle down to monitor events. Shortly, a feeling of regret overcomes you. You may have lost out on a fascinating opportunity.

As you become friendly with the Atlantean technicians, they reveal to you that they know a secret that was uncovered by the Atlanteans centuries ago. The secret, they say, involves the future of all life-forms on planet Earth.

"What is it?" you ask eagerly.

Turn to page 81.

Music fills the compartment where you and Horton sit staring at the silver capsule. The sound intensifies. Your finger moves away from the blaster button, and your arms fall to your sides, powerless. The music turns to colored lights, which fill the compartment.

A soothing voice penetrates the music.

"Thank you for allowing us aboard your vessel. We are now in control. Relax. Do not resist. Next stop, the transit station in Atlantis. Final destination, the planet Agyr."

The End

108

You push the Flood button, and seawater rapidly fills the command compartment, pushing you and Horton toward the escape hatch.

The hatch is ringed with explosive bolts. Quickly you insert a key and push a small button.

Zoom! The bolts fire, the hatch flies off, and you and Horton fight your way out into the sea. The *Seeker II* shudders and sinks further into the murky ocean.

Turn to page 100.

"One more try, Horton," you say. "I don't think those suits will survive the pressure out there."

Horton shakes his head and continues to put on the bulky gear. The *Seeker II* sinks deeper and deeper as you fiddle with the emergency power controls. Water begins to seep onto the floor plates.

Then, "Look. It's happening! The power is gaining," you cry suddenly. Your spirits rise in direct proportion to the needle indicating power gain. You concentrate your entire will on the needle, silently commanding it to keep rising. It does.

Lights come on again in the compartment. The controls, similar to airplane controls, grow firmer as you add power.

Then, as you watch with disbelieving eyes, the ocean floor falls away!

Turn to page 87.

110

Without even notifying Horton of your intentions, you grab him by the arm and pull him through what you hope is the exit from the blob

"Stop, whoever you are! Hands up! This is a security check!" commands one of the Atlanteans. He sounds just like an Earth police officer.

You glance back at Martullus, and in that second, the Atlanteans turn into energy forms. But they snap into sharp humanoid focus when you look back at them.

"We've done nothing wrong!" Horton says.

You see a blurry movement in the blob as Martullus tries to escape. His energy shape slips out but it's immediately restrained by a band of silver light.

"Martullus, number forty-four, sixty-seven twenty-eight, Atlantean subcolony, convicted of deceit and slave-trading!" announces one of the officers. "He's on our list. We have him this time. Take him to headquarters," he orders the other officers. "These two can be interrogated here. I get no reading on them from the data bank."

He turns back to you. He's not a friendly-looking person.

Turn to page 92.

"I feared that," Yangton says. "They are worse, more dangerous than the Nodoors. The Earth crafts try to destroy anything they can't control. Yours is a hostile world."

"Maybe," you reply, "but the Nodoors certainly disrupt life in Atlantis, if I remember correctly."

At that moment, the intruder sub fires a torpedo with a warhead.

"They've done it again," Moldoona says. "Activate energy deflection. Return their approach with full force. This gets so boring, you know. They will not or cannot communicate with us, so they just fire away."

"Yes, but—" Your protest is interrupted by a *whump!* as the sub's torpedo hits the energy deflectors and is returned to its point of origin where it detonates.

"That's all for them. Serves them right," Moldoona says. "Prepare to return to Atlantis."

The silver capsule sinks into the inky cloud and heads for home.

•

The End

"They want to believe that we mean no harm," Marpex informs you, "but you humans have hurt them too often. It will take time. They are lovely, intelligent creatures, but they do not really trust us."

"So what's your next step?" you ask.

"Patience and positive action to show them that we are what we say we are. We might also help them avoid Earthling whaling ships. That is under discussion right now. Thanks for being the hostage."

Now that you're safely back in Atlantis, you recall fondly the friendliness of the young whales and the sweetness of the young dolphin voices. "It was my pleasure," you reply. "It really was!"

The End

Gentle whining sounds are accompanied by the soothing music you heard when the Atlanteans made initial contact with you from their silver capsule. You feel peacefulness and tranquillity return to you.

"We're going to Atlantis! I'm finally going back to Atlantis!" you say out loud, but more to yourself than to anyone else.

The silver capsule slips into the crack in the ocean floor. Far below you see light. The light soon surrounds the capsule.

"Recovery commencing," announces the computer.

You become sleepy and doze off. When you awake, you have arrived in the Lost City of Atlantis.

The End

ABOUT THE AUTHOR

R.A. MONTGOMERY is an educator and publisher. A graduate of Williams College, he also studied in graduate programs at Yale University and New York University. After serving in a variety of administrative capacities at Williston Academy and Columbia University, he co-founded Waitsfield Summer School in 1965. Following that, Montgomery helped found a research and development firm specializing in the development of educational programs. He worked for several years as a consultant to the Peace Corps in Washington, D.C., and West Africa. He is now both a writer and a publisher.

ABOUT THE ILLUSTRATOR

George Tsui was born in Hong Kong and has studied art at Sheridan College in Oakville, Canada, and at the School of Visual Arts in New York. He is a designer and illustrator and has illustrated many movie posters and book covers. Mr. Tsui lives on Long Island with his wife and two children.